Dear Parents,

Welcome to the Scholastic Reader series. We have taken over 80 years of experience with teachers, parents, and children and put it into a program that is designed to match your child's interests and skills.

Level 1—Short sentences and stories made up of words kids can sound out using their phonics skills and words that are important to remember.

Level 2—Longer sentences and stories with words kids need to know and new "big" words that they will want to know.

Level 3—From sentences to paragraphs to longer stories, these books have large "chunks" of texts and are made up of a rich vocabulary.

Level 4—First chapter books with more words and fewer pictures.

It is important that children learn to read well enough to succeed in school and beyond. Here are ideas for reading this book with your child:

- Look at the book together. Encourage your child to read the title and make a prediction about the story.
- Read the book together. Encourage your child to sound out words when appropriate. When your child struggles, you can help by providing the word.
- Encourage your child to retell the story. This is a great way to check for comprehension.
- Have your child take the fluency test on the last page to check progress.

Scholastic Readers are designed to support your child's efforts to learn how to read at every age and every stage. Enjoy helping your child learn to read and love to read.

—Francie Alexander
Chief Education Officer
Scholastic Education

For my parents
—K.H.

Copyright © 1996 by Nancy Hall, Inc.
Fluency activities copyright © 2003 Scholastic Inc.

All rights reserved. Published by Scholastic Inc.
SCHOLASTIC, CARTWHEEL BOOKS, and associated logos are trademarks
and/or registered trademarks of Scholastic Inc.

Library of Congress Cataloging-in-Publication Data is available.

ISBN 0-439-59428-6

10 9 8 7 6 5 4 3 2 1   03 04 05 06 07

Printed in the U.S.A.   23
First printing, November 1996

Our Tea Party

by Kirsten Hall
Illustrated by Dee deRosa

Scholastic Reader — Level 1

SCHOLASTIC INC.
New York Toronto London Auckland Sydney
Mexico City New Delhi Hong Kong Buenos Aires

Oh, what fun today will be!

We will have a tea party.

Here is a cup ... a saucer, too.

Some tea for me!

Some tea for you!

Here is some honey.

Here is a spoon.

Our cookies will be ready soon!

Some tea and cookies!

Join the fun!

A tea party for everyone!

Looking On

How do the boys act while the girl is preparing the tea party?

How do the boys act at the end of the story?

Rhyming Words

Match each word on the left to a picture on the right that shows a rhyming word.

tea

spoon

honey

fun

Tea Party Time

Point to the things you might find at a tea party.
Now point to the things that you would not find at a
tea party.

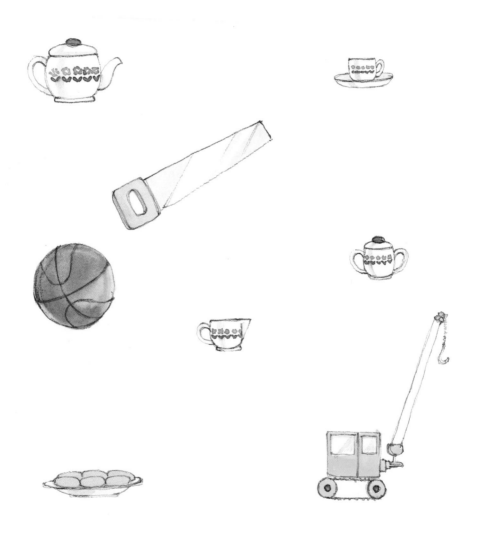

What Do You Think?

Which things could really happen? Which are make-believe?

The boy eats a cookie.

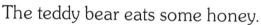

The teddy bear eats some honey.

The girl gets out of bed in the morning.

The dog picks up a teacup in its paw.

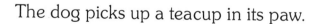

Tasty Treats

Find something sweet and crunchy.

Find something sour.

Find something sweet and sticky.

Find something salty.

Find something wet and hot.

Time for Tea

If you were planning a tea party...

Who would you invite?

Where would your guests sit?

What would you serve your guests to eat and drink?

Who would clean up when the party was over?

Answers

(Looking On)

    Answers will vary.

(Rhyming Words)

    tea

    spoon

    honey

    fun

(Tea Party Time)

    You might find:

    You would not find:

(What Do You Think?)

    These could really happen:

      The boy eats a cookie.

      The girl gets out of bed in the morning.

    These are make-believe:

      The teddy bear eats some honey.

      The dog picks up a teacup in its paw.

(Tasty Treats)

 are sweet and crunchy.

is sour.

is sweet and sticky.

are salty.

 is wet and hot.